First U.S. paperback edition 2007

The Library of Congress has cataloged the hardcover edition as follows:
Fine, Anne.
The Jamie and Angus stories / Anne Fine ;
illustrated by Penny Dale. — 1st U.S. ed.
p.   cm.
Contents: Dry-clean only — Uncle Edward teaches Angus to jump —
Flora's wedding — Tell me the story — Strawberry creams —
The perfect day.
ISBN 978-0-7636-1862-9 (hardcover)
[1. Toys — Fiction. 2. Bulls — Fiction.]
I. Title: The Jamie and Angus stories. II. Dale, Penny, ill. III. Title.
PZ7.F495673 Jam 2002
[E] — dc21   2001058117

ISBN 978-0-7636-3312-7 (paperback)

2 4 6 8 10 9 7 5 3 1

Printed in the United States of America

This book was typeset in Giovanni Book.
The illustrations were done in pencil.

Candlewick Press
2067 Massachusetts Avenue
Cambridge, Massachusetts 02140

visit us at www.candlewick.com

The Jamie and Angus Stories

Anne Fine

illustrated by Penny Dale

CANDLEWICK PRESS
CAMBRIDGE, MASSACHUSETTS

Contents

Dry-Clean Only ~ *1*

Uncle Edward Teaches Angus to Jump ~ *17*

Flora's Wedding ~ *35*

Tell Me the Story ~ *51*

Strawberry Creams ~ *65*

The Perfect Day ~ *85*

Dry-Clean Only

Jamie saw Angus staring forlornly
out of the shop window. His silky coat
looked smooth as bath water
and white as snow.

"Oh, please," begged Jamie. "Please can I have him for my birthday?"

"Your birthday was last week," Mommy said, trying to tug him past.

But Jamie wouldn't budge. "Christmas, then?"

"Christmas is not for *months*," his mother said. "By then you'll probably want something else."

"No, I won't," Jamie insisted. He pressed his nose up hard against the glass and gazed at Angus. Angus gazed at him.

"Oh, please," said Jamie. "*Please.*"

"All right," said Jamie's mother. "I'll get him. But that's what you're having for Christmas, even if you change your mind. And you're not having him even one day early."

"I'll wait," said Jamie. "I promise I won't grumble. I'll just wait."

Angus spent all autumn and half the winter stuck in a plastic bag. His head was allowed to poke out so he could breathe. He was put so high up in the cupboard that Jamie couldn't reach him. He could only wave.

But Jamie kept busy. First he made a farm
for Angus to live on. He patched fields
together from all the green and brown
scraps in the sewing basket,

painted cardboard tubes
to look like hedges,

and built several splendid
five-barred gates out of
popsicle sticks.

He made a fir tree out
of Granny's old sponge,

and a pond out of the mirror
from one of her face
powder compacts.

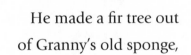

And every day he kept Angus up to date on how long they still had to wait before they could be really together properly.

When he'd finished the farm, Jamie built Angus a stall out of shoe boxes and corrugated paper. It was a bit messy, but it was the right size, had a good view of the pond, and looked very comfortable.

"I think you'll be happy in it," Jamie told Angus. "Cozy and safe on dark nights, and in storms."

Angus gazed down admiringly.

At last all the days passed. On Christmas Eve Angus disappeared from the top of the cupboard, and under the tree appeared a funny-shaped package with legs and horns, and two tiny holes punched in the snouty bit, so it could breathe.

"See you tomorrow," Jamie whispered to the package.

The package rustled its paper excitedly.

On Christmas morning Jamie opened his present
and he and Angus were together properly for the
first time. Angus adored his spacious greeny-brown
fields. He felt proud and confident behind his fine
painted hedges. He admired his pond. And he was
very, very happy in his stall. And Jamie was happy,
too. He'd waited so long to bury his face in
that magnificent silky coat, as smooth
as bath water and white as snow.

The only thing he wasn't sure about was the horrid tickly label behind Angus's ear that said DRY-CLEAN ONLY.

"What does it mean?" he asked his mother.

"It means he can't go in the washing machine," his mother explained. "If he gets grubby, he'll have to go to the dry cleaners with all my suits and fancy dresses."

Jamie knew Angus had heard. Next time they went to the cleaners, he felt him tremble in his arms. The glue smell was terrible, and the giant machines juddered and roared.

Jamie leaned closer, till the horrid label tickled his cheek. "Don't worry," he whispered in Angus's gorgeous silky white ear. "I promise you'll never, *ever* have to come here. I'll keep you clean."

Angus gazed up at him trustingly.

So, because they would never need it (and it was horrid and tickly), next time he was mending

8

one of Angus's fields, Jamie used the sewing scissors to cut off Angus's little DRY-CLEAN ONLY label and threw it in the trash.

"There," he warned Angus sternly. "Now stay clean."

But Angus couldn't. He charged over his fields so fast, he kept crashing through his hedge and sliding under the bookcase into the dust and the cobwebs. Once, when his shed was being mended, he got mixed up with all the muddy boots. And when Jamie was touching up the popsicle-stick gates, he got sticky with glue and tipped over a jar of paint.

"He's looking pretty scruffy," Mommy observed.

"Downright insanitary," said Granny.

Jamie just held Angus tighter. But one day, while Jamie was away at nursery school, Granny picked up poor Angus, frowned at the mess of dust and mud and glue and cobwebs and paint, and put him in the washing machine with the towels and the washcloths.

She poured in the powder and pressed the "on" button.

Disaster! When Angus came out, his silky white coat was gone, and in its place was a shaggy gray tangle. He didn't look like Angus at all.

He looked terrible. *Terrible!*

When Jamie came home and saw him, he burst into tears.

"Never mind." Mommy tried to comfort him. "Perhaps he'll look better when he's a bit drier."

But he didn't. If anything, he looked even worse.

"He should have had a label," Granny said. "He should have said DRY-CLEAN ONLY. Then it would never have happened."

Jamie said nothing. He just cried even harder. Angus spent that night in the kitchen. And the next.

(Mommy said he was still too damp to be anywhere else.) But on the third morning, at breakfast time, Jamie found a funny-shaped package next to his plate.

From Granny, said the label. DRY-CLEAN ONLY.

Jamie took off the wrappings while Angus watched anxiously.

"I hope you like him," said Granny. "He's exactly the same."

He was, too. His silky coat was smooth as bath water and white as snow. Jamie buried his face in it. It felt *perfect* (except for the tickly label).

Jamie took a good long look at Angus, still waiting patiently near the heater, all damp and gray and bedraggled. Then he looked at the present from Granny, all proud and silky and shining and new.

Maybe he'd be too proud to charge around the greeny-brown patch fields like Angus. Maybe he wouldn't think much of a stall made out of a shoe box. Maybe he'd laugh at the painted cardboard-tube hedges and the popsicle-stick gates. Maybe he'd think the mirror pond wasn't big enough.

Maybe he wouldn't be as happy as Angus. Or as much of a friend.

Jamie handed the lovely new present back to
Granny. "I think he should go back to the shop," he
said firmly. "So he can find someone else."

Granny looked puzzled. "I thought you wanted
one with a silky white coat."

"Yes," Jamie said. "I thought I did too. But now I
know that all I want is Angus."

Angus and Jamie still play together almost every day. Angus still loves his farm. But now that he's scruffy and grubby-looking, he can go anywhere without worrying. And when he gets absolutely disgusting, Granny puts him back in the washing machine with the towels and the washcloths and his greeny-brown fields.

He stares hopefully out of the little glass window, while Jamie fixes the stall with tape and repaints the hedges.

Both of them waiting till they can be together again. Angus and Jamie. Jamie and Angus.

Uncle Edward Teaches Angus to Jump

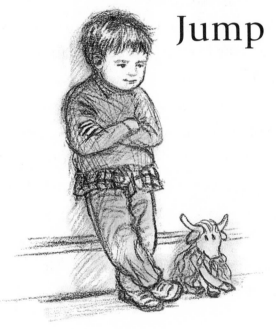

Bedtime. But Jamie really didn't
want to go upstairs.

Uncle Edward had come for a visit and Jamie didn't see why he should have to miss all the chatter and fun just because of stupid old bedtime.

"I'm not tired," he kept telling everyone.

"Maybe you're not," said his father. "But it's still bedtime, so you have to go."

"I'll take you up," said Uncle Edward. "I've never put anyone to bed before. It'll be good to start with someone like you, who knows what he's doing."

Jamie's mother laughed. "I hope you make a better job of putting Jamie to bed than you do with yourself." (Uncle Edward was famous for staying up late and not wanting to get up in the morning.)

So Jamie kissed Mommy and Daddy and took Uncle Edward's hand. "You have to say 'Up the little wooden hill to Dreamland' now," he told him.

"Do I?" said Uncle Edward.

"Yes," Jamie said.

So Uncle Edward said, "Up the little wooden hill to Dreamland," and they went up the stairs.

When they reached Jamie's room, Uncle Edward sat down on the carpet in the doorway.

"Right," he said cheerfully. "Go on, then. Get on with it."

"I thought you were supposed to be putting me to bed," said Jamie.

"No," Uncle Edward said. "You're putting yourself to bed. Angus and I are just watching." He swiveled around and put his feet halfway up one side of the doorway and balanced Angus on his stomach.

Jamie folded up his clothes and found his pajamas, and climbed over Uncle Edward and Angus to get out onto the landing to put his socks and pants in the laundry basket. Then he climbed back over them both to draw his curtains and put on his reading lamp and turn his clock to face the exact right way. Then he climbed back over Uncle Edward and Angus to go to the bathroom and brush his teeth and fill his bedside cup with fresh water.

"Aren't you coming to check that I brush my teeth properly?" he asked Uncle Edward.

"No," Uncle Edward said. "We'll soon know if you

don't, because they'll go black
and fall out much sooner than
expected."

Jamie brushed his
teeth even more properly
than usual.

When he came back, Uncle
Edward and Angus were lying
on the bed. "This is a whole lot
more comfy than that
doorway," Uncle Edward
said. "What now?"

"You read me a story,"
explained Jamie.

Uncle Edward sat up on the bed.
"I know," he said. "We'll toss for it. Heads, I read you
a story. Tails, you read one to me."

"No," Jamie insisted. "You have to read the story."

So Uncle Edward read the story. Then he switched
off the lamp. "I'm going downstairs now," he said to
Jamie. "Happy?"

"No," Jamie said, because really he wanted to be

downstairs with everybody in the chatter and the light, not stuck up in his nearly dark bedroom with Angus, the two of them all by themselves. "Can't you stay just till I go to sleep?"

"I'll half stay," offered Uncle Edward. "I'll stay in the doorway with Angus. Then I'll be half back with them and half here with you."

"All right," said Jamie, "but you must promise to remember to put Angus safely in his shoe-box stall before you leave, because that's where he sleeps."

"I won't forget," said Uncle Edward.

So Jamie shut his eyes and tried to go to sleep. After a while Uncle Edward started whistling softly.

Jamie opened his eyes. "I can't sleep if you're whistling," he scolded.

So Uncle Edward stopped whistling. Jamie shut his eyes and tried to sleep again. It was quiet for a bit, then Uncle Edward started running one of Jamie's little plastic tractors over the tiny ribs in the carpet. "*Vroom-vroom. Vroom-vroom.*"

Jamie opened his eyes. "I can't go to sleep if you keep going *vroom-vroom*," he explained.

Uncle Edward sighed. "I can't whistle and I can't go *vroom-vroom*," he said. "So what am I supposed to sit here doing?"

But Jamie didn't know, because when Mommy and Daddy and Flora the babysitter put him to bed, all they did was read him a story and then leave the door ajar so he could see a slice of warm light from the landing. None of them ever lay on their back in the doorway with their head up one side of the door and their feet up the other, and Angus standing on their stomach.

"I'm not sure," he said. "Maybe you're just supposed to lie there quietly, doing nothing."

"That's a bit dull," said Uncle Edward. "I'll tell you what. I'll spend the time usefully, teaching Angus how to jump."

Jamie sat up in bed. "Angus can't—"

"Sssh!" Uncle Edward interrupted him. "Lie down and shut your eyes. And don't say a word because Angus has to concentrate."

So Jamie lay down and pretended to shut his eyes while Uncle Edward took Angus off his stomach and

24

stood him on the carpet. "Right, Angus," he told
him. "We'll start with something really simple." He
glanced at Jamie. "You're not peeking, are you?"

"No," Jamie lied.

"Yes, you are," Uncle Edward said. "I can tell.
But you mustn't. It isn't fair to Angus. Not while
he's learning."

And Uncle Edward sailed Angus over his stomach and put him down on the carpet on the other side, where Jamie couldn't see him.

"Right," he said. "We'll begin with a little hop and a skip, just to warm up."

In the dark, Jamie heard a tiny thudding noise, as if Angus were hopping and skipping on the carpet.

"That's good," said Uncle Edward. "Well done, Angus. That's a very fine start."

Jamie sat up. "But Angus doesn't—"

"Sssh!" Uncle Edward interrupted him. "You mustn't distract Angus while he's having his lesson."

So Jamie lay down and shut his eyes again.

"Right, Angus," said Uncle Edward. "Now we'll do a backward somersault, all the way over and around. It's a challenge, but I think that you'll manage it."

There was another soft thudding noise, as if Angus were doing a backward somersault, all the way over and around.

"Excellent!" said Uncle Edward. "You're a born jumper, Angus."

Jamie sat up again, but he couldn't see anything because Uncle Edward was in the doorway. So he lay down and shut his eyes again.

"Now, Angus," said Uncle Edward. "We'll try your first head over heels roly-poly. But remember to tuck your hooves in, or you'll get all untidy and trip over them. Ready?"

Jamie listened hard. It was easier with his eyes closed. First he heard a few soft thuds along the carpet, as if Angus were cantering to get up speed. Then there was a little silent wait, as if Angus were flying head over hooves in the air. And then there was a big thud.

"Brilliant!" said Uncle Edward. "That was really good."

Jamie sat up again. "Can I watch?"

"No. Not while he's practicing. Wait till he's perfect."

So Jamie lay back and listened. Deep in the dark, with his eyes tightly closed, it was easy to see all the things he was hearing. When Uncle Edward said, "Right, Angus. Now we're going to jump off all four hooves at once, up really, really high," he could almost see Angus shooting up as fast as a rocket.

And when Uncle Edward said, "Now, how about a great fancy twirl in the air?" in his head Jamie could clearly see Angus spinning around so fast that his hooves nearly got tangled.

On and on went the lesson, with Uncle Edward's voice getting softer and softer, and the jumps getting fancier and fancier, and Angus getting more and

more perfect, till Jamie heard
Uncle Edward whispering,
"And now, Angus, we're going
to do an amazing, astonishing,
wonderful double fancy
backward bounce with treble spin

and extra twirl; and after that I
want you to just keep rising up
as high and high as you can
go — up, up, and up . . ."
And, with his eyes still
tightly closed, Jamie saw
Angus do one last amazing,
astonishing, wonderful
double fancy backward
bounce with treble

spin and extra twirl, and
then rise up as smoothly
and calmly and perfectly
as a let-go balloon, up,
up and up, almost as
high as the ceiling,

29

then out of the open window on the landing
and up some more, into the shadowy blue
moonlit sky, up, up and up, on and on, higher and
higher, till he was floating over silvered clouds,
floating and floating and floating
and floating . . .

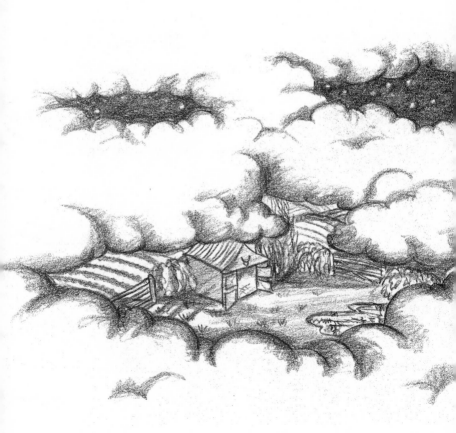

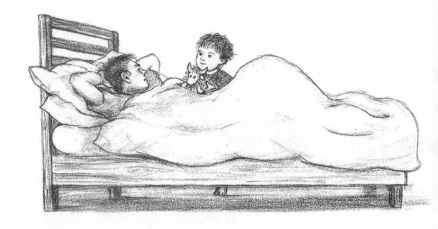

In the morning, when Jamie woke up, he saw Angus standing safely in his stall, not looking any different from usual, except that on his hooves were tiny specks of fluff, the same color as the carpet on the landing.

Jamie carried him through to where Uncle Edward was sleeping and plonked him on the bed.

"Go on," challenged Jamie. "Show me. Now that he's finished practicing, show me how Angus can jump."

Uncle Edward opened one eye and groaned. "Go on, then," he told Angus. "Now that you're perfect, show him. Jump."

Angus just stood there with carpet fluff on his hooves.

"See?" Jamie said. "Angus can't—"

"Sssh!" Uncle Edward interrupted. "You mustn't say anything to upset him. It's just that he's forgotten. You know what this means, don't you? It means I'll have to put you to bed again tonight, to give him another lesson."

And, thinking he'd enjoy that more than arguing, Jamie left poor tired Uncle Edward to sleep and went down to have breakfast with Mommy and Daddy.

Flora's Wedding

Flora the babysitter
was going to get married.

She had a white dress with pretend pearls embroidered all over it. She had the prettiest satin slippers. And she had two daisy barrettes to hold back her tumbling hair.

And she wanted to have her wedding party in a field full of buttercups.

"Suppose it rains," said Jamie's mother.

"It won't rain," said Flora.

"Won't it be difficult to get the wedding cake safely into the field?" asked Jamie's father.

"No," Flora told him. "Even fields have gates."

"Angus will like it," said Jamie. "Angus loves fields. And he'll especially like a field full of buttercups."

So as soon as Jamie's mother and father had kissed Jamie good-bye and gone out, Flora and Jamie sat down and made Angus his very own invitation:

After the wedding,
come to the Buttercup Field
with everyone
for a Grand Party
(with special flyaway wishing balloons)

"What's a special flyaway wishing balloon?" asked
Jamie.

"It's a balloon with a special wish written on it,"
said Flora.

"And does it really fly away?" asked Jamie.

"Oh, yes," said Flora.

"How high?" asked Jamie.

"Wait and see," said Flora.

So Jamie waited. He waited while Flora and her
boyfriend Mark stood at the front of the church
and promised to love one another forever and ever.

He waited while all the ladies
in hats dabbed at their tears with their
hankies and hurried down the steps to the
pavement. And he waited while all the people
who didn't want to walk over the hill to the party
took a seat in the minibus.

Then all the rest of them set off walking in a long
straggly line, down the lane, through the wood,
and over the hill toward Flora's field of buttercups.
Jamie had Angus in his backpack, with his head
sticking out so Angus could see where they'd been,
and when they reached the top of the hill he turned
around so Angus could see where they were going.

"I certainly hope the wedding cake gets there
safely," said Jamie's father.

"I hope the rain holds off," said Jamie's mother.

Then everyone straggled down the hill in a long
line and into the field of buttercups.

It was a wonderful party. First Angus got covered in puffy yellow pollen from prancing through all the buttercups. Then, when Jamie had shaken that off, he got covered in petals from playing under the hawthorn hedges.

Jamie made a daisy-chain necklace for Flora, to go with her daisy barrettes.

Everyone loved the cake, which had reached the field safely (just as Flora had said it would).

And the rain held off (just as Flora had said it would).

Then Flora called everyone around her. "We're going to make our special flyaway balloon wishes now."

Out from behind the hedge came a floating mountain of shiny colored balloons, all straining to escape up into the bright blue sky. Underneath was Mark, carefully holding the strings tight. He handed everyone a huge fat glossy balloon on a string. Daddy had a green one. Mommy's was purple. And the one he gave Jamie was buttercup yellow.

"Can Angus have one?" begged Jamie. "Can he have a red one, please? Red is his favorite color. Angus really, really loves red balloons."

Mark looked down at Angus, tucked under Jamie's arm. "Did Angus get a proper invitation?" he asked. "Or did he just come along with you?"

"He had a proper invitation," Jamie told him. "Flora and I made it together when she came last time."

And the words "last time" made him feel sad, because now that Flora was married, maybe she wouldn't ever come to babysit for him again.

Mark saw his sad face and picked one of the red balloons out of his giant floating mountain.

"Angus can have his own balloon because there are exactly the same number of balloons as invitations.

And he can have a red one. I'll tie it safely around one of his legs." Mark tied a double bow, just to be sure.

"Now you hang on to Angus," he warned Jamie, "in case he floats up in the air with his balloon."

Jamie held Angus tighter. "Can you give me a double bow on my balloon as well?" he asked Mark.

"All right," said Mark, and tied the other balloon to Jamie's arm.

So now Jamie was standing in the circle with his own fat shiny yellow balloon floating up from one arm, and Angus tucked under the other arm with his fat shiny red balloon floating up from him.

Flora went around the circle with felt pens. "Make a wish," she told everyone. "Write it on the balloon."

Jamie asked Mommy, "Can I please wish to take my balloon home after the party?"

Mommy gave Jamie a little look. "Do you think the wish can come true," she asked, "if the balloon doesn't fly away?"

Jamie thought for a little. "Yes," he said firmly. "Yes. I think it can."

Mommy didn't argue. She went rushing off to hold Aunt Lilian's balloon while she wrote her wish on it.

"Maybe it can," agreed Daddy, hurrying off to hold Uncle Tony's balloon steady for him. "But I don't think you're supposed to be wishing for yourself."

Jamie looked around at all the people in the buttercup field, racking their brains to think of special wedding day wishes for Flora and Mark.

"Health!" Flora's mother was saying.

"Wealth!" said Aunt Lilian.

"Four bouncing babies!" suggested Uncle Tony.

"Perfect happiness!" said Mark's best friend.

"Long lives together!" said Flora's sister.

"A car that starts all through the winter!" said the pastor.

Jamie and Angus looked at one another. Jamie knew what Angus was thinking. And Angus knew what Jamie was thinking.

When Mark came over to help Angus and Jamie write their wishes, Jamie said, "I wish that Angus doesn't have to let go of his beautiful fat red balloon, because he really, really, really loves balloons — especially red ones."

So Mark wrote that on Jamie's yellow balloon. Then he looked at Angus. "What about you?" he said. "What's your special flyaway wish for someone else?"

Angus looked shy.

"What Angus wishes," said Jamie, "is that, even though Flora is married to you now, she'll still sometimes come back to babysit for me."

"Really?" said Mark. "Is that so?" And in case Jamie's wish for Angus came true, and Angus didn't have to let his beautiful red balloon float away with all the others, Mark wrote Angus's wish for Jamie under Jamie's wish for Angus on the yellow one.

"Right," he said. "And now I'd better go and nibble the bride's ear, just like it says in the marriage rules."

Jamie watched him go back to Flora. After
a moment he turned to Angus and told him,
"It doesn't look to me as if Mark's nibbling.
To me it looks more as if he's whispering."

But Angus was staring at buttercups and
paying no attention.

"Time to let go of the balloons," said Flora a few minutes later. "Except for Angus's red one, which has to stay on earth for luck." She turned to Jamie. "If he doesn't mind."

"Oh, no," said Jamie. "He won't mind. He'll be quite pleased really."

"That's what I thought," said Flora. And she smiled.

Then everyone stood in a circle in the buttercups. Jamie's father untied the double bow on Jamie's arm, so the yellow balloon could go sailing up with the others. Jamie held the string tightly.

"One, two, three—go!" cried Flora, and everyone let go. Except for Angus's red one, all the balloons floated up, up, carrying their good wishes over the trees and up to the clouds — sky-high! And then everyone cheered and went on with the party.

Flora's been married for months now. But she still comes to babysit every now and again. Sometimes she brings Mark. Sometimes she doesn't. But she always brings a balloon because Angus really, really loves them — especially red ones.

And Jamie quite likes red ones too.

Tell Me the Story

"Tell me the story of how I grew
out of my stroller."

Daddy reeled around the bedroom, clutching his head. "Oh, no. Not again! I've told you a million, billion times."

"So, this time, tell Angus."

Daddy sank onto the end of the bed, and Jamie tucked Angus in neatly beside him under the covers, with just his eyes and nose and front hooves sticking out.

"Quite sure he's comfy?" Daddy asked.

"Yes. Go on with the story."

Daddy turned to Angus. "Well, Angus. This is how it happened. Young Jamie here was getting on for nearly four whole years old—"

"I was three and a half," Jamie corrected him.

"Who's telling this story?" Daddy asked. "You, or me?"

"You," Jamie said.

"And who am I telling?"

"Angus."

"Right," Daddy said. "So don't interrupt."

And he went back to the tale of how Jamie grew out of his stroller.

"So, one day, as a treat for Granny's birthday, we all went on a visit to the Museum of Modern Art."

"You know Granny likes art," Jamie reminded Angus. "That's why she paints her own pictures and makes her own clay pots and bowls, and bends all sorts of odd bits of metal into fancy shapes to keep on her patio. And on Thursdays she even goes to college to teach other people how to do it."

"Wednesdays," said Jamie's father. "On Thursdays she takes you swimming."

"Who was telling that bit?" asked Jamie. "You, or me?"

"You were," said Daddy.

"And who was I telling?"

"Angus."

"That's right," said Jamie. And he waited for his father to get on with the story.

Daddy climbed into bed next to Angus, to be a little warmer and comfier, and carried on.

"So off we all went — Jamie and Granny and Mommy and me. And Jamie was sitting in his battered old stroller. And the museum is right at the top of the hill. So guess who had to push Jamie in his stroller all the way up to the top?"

There was a silence.

Jamie put his head down, close to Angus's snout.

"Angus guesses that you did," he told his father.

"And Angus is dead right!" said Daddy. "I had to push that great big fat lazy tub of lard called Jamie all the way up the hill to the museum."

"I wasn't a great big fat lazy tub of lard," Jamie assured Angus. "I was perfectly normal. It's just that my legs were tired."

"Your legs weren't tired," said Daddy. "You just liked being pushed. You just liked sitting there, all comfy in your battered and rusty old stroller, with your thumb in your mouth, watching the world go by."

Jamie sat quietly for a while, remembering sitting all comfy in his battered and rusty old stroller, with his thumb in his mouth, watching the world go by.

"*I* was the one with tired legs," Daddy grumbled to Angus. "And tired arms. And tired back. And tired every bit of me."

"Go on with the story," said Jamie.

Daddy got on with the story. "So then we trailed Granny all the way around the great big Museum of Modern Art," he explained to Angus. "First we went through the rooms with all the big splotches. Then we went through the rooms with all the clotty lumps. And then we went outside in the gardens to look at all the clumps of tangled metal."

"Don't listen to him," Jamie said to Angus. "He says it that way to tease Granny. But Granny says what he *means* is that we went through the rooms with all the lovely modern paintings, and then through the rooms with all the interesting pottery, and then out in the gardens to look at all the amazing metal sculptures."

"And I know you'll find this hard to believe, Angus," Daddy said. "But, the whole time,

57

this great big fat lazy tub of lard sitting here in the bed beside you wouldn't get out of his stroller, even though he was getting on for nearly four whole years old."

"Three and a half," corrected Jamie. "And Daddy's just being rude. He does it to tease me."

Daddy turned to Angus. "And then we went home. And, even then, this great big fat lazy lump wouldn't get out of his stroller and walk for a little bit. Even though it was downhill all the way."

"I was tired," said Jamie.

"You were lazy," said Daddy.

Angus gazed ahead sadly.

"Yes," Daddy said. "It's a shocking story, Angus, isn't it? And it gets *worse*."

Angus's eyes were very wide.

"Only because Daddy got cross and lost his temper," Jamie explained to Angus.

"Who's telling this bit of the story?" asked Daddy.

"You are," said Jamie.

"So I got cross," said Daddy. "I'd pushed this great fat lazy tub of lard all the way up the hill. And I'd pushed him all the way around the museum and the gardens. And now I was having to push him all the way back down the hill again."

"Pull me, he means," explained Jamie. "To stop the stroller from running away with me down the hill."

"And by the time we got to Granny's house, my arms were aching even worse than my legs and my back," Daddy explained to Angus. "And still Jamie wouldn't get out and walk. So when we reached our own gate, I said to him, 'You can at least get out now and walk up your own garden path.'"

He leaned down to Angus. "And do you know what this precious Jamie of yours said?"

Angus waited on tenterhooks.

"He said, 'No!' Can you believe that, Angus? Getting on for nearly four whole years old—"

"Three and a half," corrected Jamie.

"And he just said, 'No!' Good thing you weren't there, Angus. You'd have been shocked. Someone of that age, refusing to get out of their battered and rusty old stroller and walk up their own garden path."

Angus looked shocked.

"So I did what anybody would have done, Angus. I lost my temper. I tipped this great big fat lazy tub of lard out onto the grass, and I stamped on that rusty and battered old stroller over and over till it was just a heap of tangled metal, and nobody was ever going to be able to sit in it ever again."

"There," Jamie said proudly. "That is the story of how I grew out of my stroller."

Daddy got out from under the covers and kissed Jamie, shook hand and hoof with Angus, and switched off the bedside lamp.

"Aren't you going to tell Angus the very end of the story before you go downstairs to Mommy?" Jamie asked.

Daddy hurried to the door. "No."

"I'll tell him, then," warned Jamie. "After you've gone."

Daddy shook a finger. "Don't you listen to him, Angus. He'll only be saying it to tease me."

And off he went downstairs to Mommy.

In the dark, Jamie told Angus the very end of the story. How Granny had come over the next morning

60

and seen the tangly mess of battered, rusty, stamped-on stroller and said to Daddy, "Oh, look! I knew you only said you didn't like modern art to tease me! Now I see you've even made a lovely bit of it all on your own in your very own garden."

And she'd taken it home before the garbage men got it, and she kept it on her patio to tease him back.

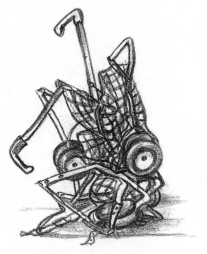

Temper, Temper!
by Jamie's father
(Rusty metal and webbing)

Strawberry
Creams

Jamie had a stomachache.

"Where, exactly?" Mommy asked, giving him a little prod.

"Ouch!" Jamie told her.

Next day it was no better, so they went down to the clinic, where Nurse asked Jamie if she could take a look.

"Where, exactly?" she asked him, pressing his stomach.

"Ouch!" Jamie told her.

Nurse sent him in to Dr. Helen.

"Where, exactly?" she asked, leaning over to press gently all around his belly button.

"Ouch!" Jamie told her. "Ouch, ouch, *ouch*!" (He was getting fed up with all this prodding and pressing.)

In the end Dr. Helen told Mommy, "I think we're going to have to bring him in."

Where, exactly? thought Jamie. He looked anxiously at Angus and Angus looked anxiously back at him. "Can Angus come with me?" he asked.

"Of course," said Dr. Helen.
"As long as he knows how
to keep his horns to himself
in bed, and to keep quiet
when other people are
sleeping."

So Jamie and Angus went into the hospital. Jamie
had brand-new pajamas with giant froggy pockets,
and Angus wore a ribbon around his neck with a
label giving Jamie's name and ward number (which
was 17). They had a bed by the window. In the next
bed was Mahailia, who had long black hair, pink
pajamas, a huge box of chocolates and an enormous,
fat stuffed seal called Nafisa.

"What's wrong with you, then?" Jamie's mother
asked.

In answer, Mahailia lifted up her pajama top
to show them a neat line of tiny stitches right across
her tummy.

"This," she said. "But I'm much better now." And
as soon as her mother and father had gone back
home to look after her sister, she wandered off to
watch television in a little room with glass walls at
the end of the ward.

Jamie played cards with Mommy. And then he let Daddy read him a story. And then he said to his parents, "You can go home now, too, if you like."

"That's all right," Daddy said. "We're happy to stay with you."

"Oh," Jamie said.

So he played cards with Daddy. And then he let Mommy read him a story. And then he tried again. "You can go home now, if you like."

"Certainly not," Daddy said.

But Mommy was looking at Jamie, and suddenly she grinned and said, "Would you and Angus like Daddy and me to go home so you can watch TV with Mahailia?"

"Yes, please," said Jamie. "But don't forget to come back in the morning."

So Mommy and Daddy went home, and Jamie wandered down the ward to the room at the end with the glass walls. He stood in the doorway for a while, watching the TV. Then he changed his mind and went back to his own bed to play cards with Angus and read him a story.

Then Mahailia came back and sat on his bed,
and they played cards in two teams: Angus and
Jamie versus Nafisa and Mahailia.

"I'd give you one of my chocolates," Mahailia told
Jamie afterward. "But I'm keeping the last ones
specially for the day when they tell me that I can go
home again."

Then she got back in her own bed and went to
sleep.

Jamie and Angus played cards a little longer, and
Jamie couldn't help noticing that Angus kept looking
at the big box of chocolates on top of Mahailia's
bedside table.

Perhaps he was curious about how many she was keeping specially for the day when they told her that she could go home again. After all, it was a big box. Jamie thought Mahailia wouldn't mind if Angus was allowed to lift the lid a tiny bit with his nose — just to take a quick peek.

Jamie held Angus up, and Angus lifted the edge of the lid with his nose. Inside was a sea of empty brown wrappers, but only three chocolates left.

Only three.

Three . . .

Three she was keeping specially.

Jamie thought Angus might want to know what sort they were, in case they were the kind that he didn't like anyway. But they were all strawberry creams, and Angus really did like strawberry creams. (So did Jamie.)

Angus didn't mean to help Jamie choose one.

And he certainly didn't mean to help Jamie take it.

Or eat it.

It was just that Angus
and Jamie weren't used to being
in hospital. And Jamie wasn't used to
being in a strange bed. And he certainly wasn't
used to having someone else's box of chocolates
so close that the last three could practically jump
into his mouth. All three!

Three she was keeping specially.

Next morning Jamie woke up feeling terrible.
Terrible! And it wasn't just the stomachache. He
peeked around to see if Mahailia was already
pointing her finger at him, ready to say, "You stole
my last three chocolates!"

But she wasn't there!

One of the nurses saw him staring at the empty
bed. "Don't look so worried," she told him.
"Mahailia's just gone to have her stitches out
because she's going home today."

Going home? Jamie looked guiltily at Angus, and Angus looked guiltily back at him. They were in trouble now. As soon as Mahailia came back, she'd look in her chocolate box and find it empty.

Jamie was still sitting worrying when his mother came. She gave him a hug and said, "My word, you look miserable!"

He couldn't help it — he burst into tears.

Mommy hugged him tighter. "Shall I read you a story?"

Jamie shook his head.

"Shall I play cards with you?"

Jamie shook his head again.

"Well, shall I go off and find the lady with the little shop on wheels, and buy you a brand-new fancy coloring book and a nice pack of felt pens?"

And because he was fed up with shaking his head, Jamie found himself nodding.

While his mother was gone, Dr. Helen arrived with a crowd of young doctors in white coats carrying clipboards and pens.

"Good morning, Jamie," she said to him. "Today

73

I've brought a whole gang to look at your very interesting tummy."

There they all were: short doctors, tall doctors, pink doctors, brown doctors, lady doctors, men doctors, cheerful doctors, worried doctors. They stood in a circle round his bed, looking at Jamie until he felt even *worse*.

"May I?" asked Dr. Helen, and she reached down to lift his pajama top with the giant froggy pockets.

Not so politely, Jamie tugged it down again.

"I expect you're fed up with everyone wanting to prod your stomach," said Dr. Helen. "But it's a shame, because all these young doctors here could learn quite a lot from just one little press."

Jamie just scowled and tugged his pajama top down even farther.

"Please?" Dr. Helen asked. "We're only here to help."

But Jamie wasn't in the mood for "please." He was about as fed up as a body can be. He was sick of having a stomachache. He was cross with himself for eating Mahailia's last three strawberry creams, and he was worried that, when she found out, she'd think he and Angus were mean and horrible, and not to be trusted. And he was sick of everyone standing around wanting to lift his pajama top to press him and prod him.

Suddenly Jamie had an idea to make them all go away at once.

He raised his pajama top. "All right," he told them. "But you'll have to pay. And it's expensive. It's a penny a press and two pennies a prod."

And he waited for them to move on to another bed, to someone who wasn't so rude and ungrateful.

Dr. Helen waggled a finger. "It was free yesterday," she reminded him.

"That was a special offer," Jamie told her firmly. "And it's over now."

He sat in his bed with his arms folded, waiting for them to move off. But no one did. First they all looked at one another. Then one or two of them started grinning. And the young man who was nearest rooted deep in the pockets of his white coat, searching for coins.

Finding a penny, he held it out. "I'll have a little press, please."

What could poor Jamie do now? He wasn't allowed to take money from strangers! He shook his head. But instead of dropping the coin back in his pocket, the doctor laid it on the bedside cabinet, right between Angus's front hooves.

Jamie gave up. He'd made a bargain so he had to

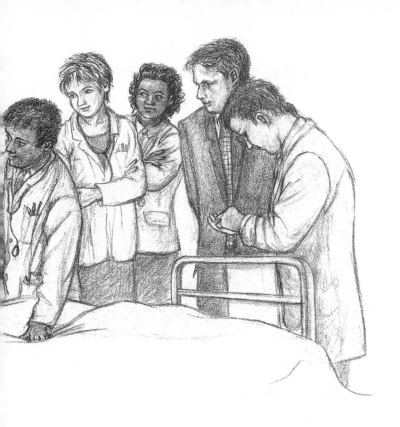

keep it. Sighing, he lifted his pajama top and waited
to be peered at and pressed and prodded.

The young man leaned over and gave Jamie's
stomach a very gentle little press. "Mmmmm!" he
said. "Now that *is* interesting."

Another doctor fished deep in her pocket and put
two pennies down in front of Angus. "If it's that
interesting, I'll have a prod, please."

Jamie felt guilty, seeing the pennies between Angus's hooves. So he said, "You can have a free press too."

"Bargain!" said the doctor. And, once she'd finished, she told everyone, "That was worth every penny, if you want my opinion."

So then all of them wanted a go at pressing and prodding. The pile of pennies between Angus's hooves grew higher and higher. Some had to borrow from their mates. Some came back for seconds. And one of them even fetched out her checkbook.

"I'm afraid Angus doesn't accept checks," said Jamie. "Or Visa. Or Mastercard."

So that doctor had a free turn. By the end, every last one of them had had a turn, and all agreed that Jamie's was, without a doubt, the most interesting stomach any of them had ever paid to press.

And then they all moved off down the ward to look at someone else. Jamie slid out of bed and scooped the money into his giant froggy pockets just as his mother and the lady with the shop on wheels came through the swinging doors.

While his mother was
busy talking to Dr. Helen,
Jamie asked the lady,
"Please, do you have any
strawberry creams?"

She rooted through her packets. "Lemon — and coffee — and — yes! — you're in luck. Here's a packet of strawberry creams."

"How many are there?" asked Jamie.

She counted through the plastic wrap. "Five."

"Goody!" said Jamie. He scooped all the money out of his pajama pockets into her hands, and together they counted it.

"Just enough!" she said.

Quickly he took the packet. While Angus watched him anxiously, Jamie lifted the lid of Mahailia's box and tipped in three chocolates. Then he put the lid back on safely and climbed into bed again. He was still

80

sitting, good as gold, playing cards with his mother, when Mahailia came back to show him the marks where they'd taken out her stitches.

Jamie stayed in hospital for six whole days. He finished the coloring book and used up the felt pens. Everyone visited — Granny and Flora and even Uncle Edward — and everyone kept asking why, even after the doctors had fixed his stomachache, he still wouldn't eat the two strawberry creams on top of his bedside table.

"Angus and I are saving them specially," he kept having to explain to them, "for the day we go home again."

The Perfect Day

Jamie leaned over the arm of the sofa
and dipped his finger into Daddy's drink.
Then he sucked it and made his
"that-tastes-horrible" face.

"Is it *true*," he asked, "that grown-ups like drinking
that stuff more than they like drinking Hairy Joe's
Jungle Juice?"

"Yes, I'm afraid a good number of us do,"
admitted Daddy.

Jamie took an olive out of the dish on the arm
of the sofa and nibbled the end till his mouth went
all puckery.

"And is it *true* that grown-ups like this nasty sour green taste more than they like Mr. Munchie Monster Mashdrops?"

"Yup," said his father. "And if you're not planning on finishing that olive, you can give it to me rather than waste it." He opened his mouth wide and Jamie popped the olive in. Then Jamie and Angus lay on their backs on the sofa beside Daddy, with their legs pointing up to the ceiling.

"And is it *true*," Jamie asked, "that grown-ups prefer sitting the right way up in chairs?"

"Indeed they do," said Daddy. "Except, perhaps, for Uncle Edward." He glanced at the clock on the mantelpiece. "Isn't it getting to be your bedtime?"

"No," Jamie said, and drifted through to the other room, where Mommy was busy with her papers.

He rested his elbows on the desk and watched for a bit.

"Sleepy?" Mommy asked him.

"No."

"It's almost your bedtime."

"No, it isn't," said Jamie. Then he asked, "Is it *true* that grown-ups are happy to go upstairs to bed almost as soon as it's time?"

Mommy looked at Jamie over her glasses.

"Jamie," she told him, "I'd go back to bed practically straight after breakfast if I could. And sleep for a whole week."

"A whole *week*?"

"Absolutely."

Jamie stared for a while in amazement. Then, in case the word "sleep" had reminded her, he went back to Daddy, who was watching the news, which was people droning on about banks, shares, and money.

"Is it *true*," Jamie asked him, "that grown-ups like watching the news more than they like watching Piggily-Pig cartoons?"

"Well, I do," sighed Daddy. "Whenever I get the opportunity to do so without interruption." He glanced at the clock again. "Are you *sure* it's not your bedtime?"

Jamie hurried back to the other room. "And is it *true*," he asked, "that grown-ups prefer to stay on the path in the park, and not walk with their arms out along the tops of walls, and not stamp in puddles in their boots, or make ice squeak with their shoes?"

"All true," said Mommy. "Unless you're counting Uncle Edward as a grown-up, which personally I wouldn't."

Jamie went back to Daddy. "And is it *true*," he asked, "that grown-ups don't really care much for being held upside down, or swung around really fast?"

"Gospel truth," said his father. "And a goodly number of us could live quite happily without swings, merry-go-rounds, ghost trains, or slides in the swimming pool."

"Not without *slides*?" said Jamie.

"Yes," his father assured him. "Some of us could most particularly do without slides."

He looked at the clock again.

"*And* without people who are still hanging around ten minutes after their bedtime."

So Jamie went off to bed. On the way up the stairs he said to Angus, "Tomorrow, for one day only, as an experiment, I'm going to give myself a grown-up's perfect day."

Angus just stared.

In the morning when Daddy came in to wake him, Jamie buried his head in the pillow just like Mommy and said, "I'm *exhausted*. I could sleep for a *week*."

"What was that?" said his father. "I can't hear you. You're all muffled."

Jamie lifted his head from the pillow and said it more clearly. "I could sleep for a week."

"Tough," said his father. "Now hop out of bed and put on these clothes. Pronto."

Jamie looked at the cheerful blue trousers his father was laying out for him — not exactly a grown-up's perfect color.

"Have I got anything a bit more *gray*?"

His father peered in the cupboard. "We have purple. And dark red. Bottle-green. And stripy."

"Oh, well," said Jamie. And he chose the bottle-green, because that was a color he'd seen on Uncle Edward.

While he was dressing, Jamie explained to Angus, "I shan't be talking to you quite so much today. Grown-ups don't do that. I know Daddy sometimes says 'Good morning, Angus' as he walks past you. And Mommy often says things like 'Oh, Angus, how come you fetched up *there*?' or 'How on earth did you get so grubby?' But they don't really *talk* to you—not like I do. And so I'm afraid, for you, today's going to be pretty quiet."

And Angus understood, though you could tell from the look on his face that he didn't really like it and he wasn't really happy.

At breakfast Angus watched as Jamie ate his boiled egg and then turned the shell over carefully in the eggcup and reached for a felt pen to draw some straggly hair and a grumpy face.

Then Angus watched as Jamie put the felt pen down again.

"Grown-ups don't draw on their eggs," explained Jamie, before remembering he wasn't really talking to Angus today. He could tell Angus thought it was a waste of a good shell, but he didn't say more. He just slid off his chair to get all his things ready.

On the way through the park, Jamie kept to the path. He walked around the puddles and didn't balance on the tops of walls, and they arrived even before Mrs. Hardy had opened the big doors.

Perhaps that's why grown-ups do it that way, thought Jamie (though he personally didn't think arriving early was worth it).

Since Angus wasn't there to watch, he took a break from having a grown-up's perfect day till it was time to go.

Granny had come to pick him up to take him

swimming. As they walked out, he asked her, "What would I be talking to you about now if I were a grown-up?"

"The weather?" suggested Granny. "Just perhaps for a moment, until we got started."

"All right," said Jamie. He had a think and then said conversationally, "I reckon it's getting a little bit black over Bill's mother's."

Granny stared.

"I got that from Lucy," said Jamie. "She learned it from Arif. He says it means it's going to rain."

"Honestly!" said Granny. "The things you lot pick up!"

And since she suddenly sounded grown-up enough for two, Jamie reckoned he could take a break and talk about Piggily-Pig.

At the pool, Granny asked, "Which slide for starters?"

"Neither," said Jamie. "Slides don't appeal today."

"Really?"

"Yes, really."

"Fancy!" said Granny, and joined the line for the curly one.

When they got home, Mommy said, "Tonight, for supper, there's a choice. SpaghettiOs, or what we're having, which has olives in it."

Jamie sighed. Angus was looking at him most

forlornly. He'd had a boring time alone at home, and now, instead of being cuddled and talked to and offered his very own SpaghettiO to balance on his nose, he was going to have to carry on standing by the plate rack, all alone, watching Jamie struggle through some fancy supper with olives.

But this was an experiment. It was supposed to be a grown-up's perfect day.

"I'll have what you're having," Jamie said sadly. "But only a little. Not that much."

Even though Daddy kept trading lumps of buttered bread for Jamie's piles of olive bits, Jamie was still hungry after supper. Mommy said he could have something from the jar.
He dipped his hand in.
There were Spinny Wheels
and Coconut Glories and
Peppermint Hoolas.

Then he remembered.
He took his hand out.
"I'll just have a nice fresh
orange," he said wistfully.

After supper Jamie was sent for his bath. Grown-ups don't play in baths, so he left Angus standing by the plate rack, looking lonely, and went upstairs with heavy heart.

"Bubbles?" Daddy offered.

Did grown-ups have bubbles? Sometimes they did.

But what was the point of bubbles

if Angus wasn't there

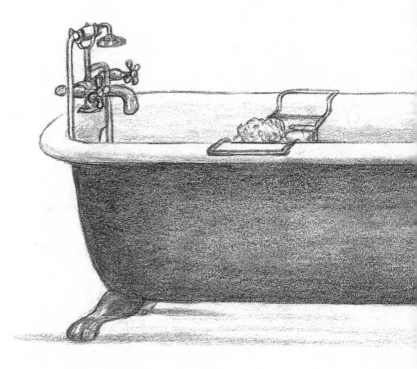

to admire Bubble Mountain's giant bubbly peaks,
and Bubble Monster's fat white bubbling hands,
and Jamie's special Bubble Soup, and the little lakes
in Bubble Land?

"No thanks," said Jamie. "I don't think I'll bother."

Jamie sat in his bath. He was bored. He was
hungry. He was lonely. And he had things
he wanted to tell Angus.

And then he realized. This was a grown-up's perfect day. So he could choose his own bedtime.

Jamie let out the water and wrapped himself up in his towel and went downstairs.

"I'm turning in now," he told Mommy, just like Daddy did.

Mommy glanced at the clock. "Really?"

"Yes," Jamie said. "It's been a long and tiring day." (That was what she often said.)

"And now I
think I'll hit the road
and have an early night."
(That was his granny.)

"I want to be really
on top in the morning."
(That was Flora, when she
didn't want his parents
to stay out late.)

99

He tried to think of something Uncle Edward might ever have said about going to bed early. But nothing came to mind.

"Right," he said, picking up Angus. "I'll just put this away tidily in my bedroom."

He could tell Angus didn't care much for being called "this." Or for being tidied.

But things were desperate.

Jamie put Angus tidily away in his shoe box shed and got into bed. Mommy brought him some cocoa to make up for the olives and read him a story. Then she turned out the light and left the door open.

Jamie told the air around him (but mostly Angus), "That is the last grown-up's perfect day I'm ever having till I'm grown up properly. Tomorrow I'm going straight back to living my own way."

He wasn't sure, but through the darkness he thought he heard the noise a little Highland bull would make if it were sighing with relief.

"Tomorrow," Jamie told the air around him (but mostly Angus), "we will have our own perfect day — I promise."

And, next day,
that is exactly
what they had.
Angus and Jamie.
Jamie and Angus.

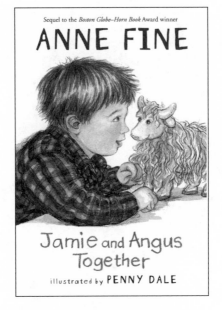

Jamie and Angus Together

by Anne Fine
illustrated by Penny Dale

Hardcover ISBN 978-0-7636-3374-5